MW00878442

The Sea of Grass

by Amy Moses

MODERN CURRICULUM PRESS

Pearson Learning Group

The evening sky is hazy and hangs like a curtain over the grasslands. Dusk is an eerie time here. A herd of zebras dissolves into the distance, the wind whistles through the grass, and a solitary zebra stomps its foot. *Whoosh. Rumble.*

The herd is gone, and as the dust from the stampede settles, I see a new cloud rising, spinning off the road. It's small and strong. To find out what's making it, I close my eyes and open my ears.

I hear the grinding of a gear shift. It is the old bus that carries my parents back to our village. A peculiar feeling wells up in my stomach—a cross between excitement and dread.

"Mom, Dad," I hear myself calling. I feel my legs carrying me to them, yet all the while, I can't figure out what is making me run.

This is my first trip to Africa. Everything is different here, and everything seems amazing. The animals I've only seen in zoos are regular visitors to the Maasai village that I'm supposed to call home while we're here.

When we first arrived in Kenya, Kisululu picked us up at the airport. Kisululu is a Maasai and my parents' guide and friend.

The Maasai have always lived in Africa. Originally, they lived in northeastern Africa, but that was about four hundred years ago. No one knows exactly why, but they moved south and settled in the grasslands of Kenya and Tanzania. They keep cattle and follow their herds to new grazing land after the grass in each spot has been eaten.

My parents, who have been coming to Africa for years, told me all about the area before we came here.

When I was little, I used to cry when they left,
then I just got used to it. It was as if they were going
to camp or something. When my parents left, my
grandparents would come and stay with me.

This time, though, I was old enough to go to Africa
with them. As I sit here, I think about home and worry
about Grandpa. My grandmother died a few months
ago, and I don't know what Grandpa is going to do
without Grandma and me.

I have a journal where I'm supposed to write down all my thoughts and feelings. I even have colored pencils for drawing. The pages keep filling up, but I still feel empty.

I have a few books to read, but here, people don't read stories to each other. They tell them! They have kept their stories alive by relating them to their children, generation after generation. I don't really see books anywhere. In fact, many of the older people are more worried about what will happen if the children learn to read than if they don't, which is so different from home!

I've decided to write a story, one that helps me make sense of all the things I see and feel. I want to tell my story, but there is no one here to tell it to.

My story will tell what it's like to live in a sea of grass. It will describe the sounds that come from the wind and the sounds that come from the animals too.

I would probably start my story like this: I am in Africa and am running at dusk through a sea of grass toward my parents.

I am living in a land where people follow animals, their cattle, goats, and sheep. Their herds lead them to where the grass and the water are plentiful. These herds, though, are not the only grazers out here.

There are wildebeest and impalas, zebras and exotic giraffes. There are also the animals that hunt them—the lions and cheetahs, hyenas and wild dogs. The grasslands are home to all of them. Water and grass are the life support of every living thing out here.

As I spend my time here, I hope to finish my story.

My parents are conservationists who are here to make sure that resources will remain for many years—for the people, animals, and plants. My parents establish wildlife refuges. It used to be that the parks were made for the animals. Many years ago, a tribe of Maasai was moved out of a crater they were living in so only animals could live there. Now we know that people need to be looked after too. At first, native people lost their homes because cities were built on their land, then they moved because the land was needed for wildlife refuges. Today the conservationists are figuring out ways for the native people to keep their traditional way of life—even as the cities spread and people of other cultures move in. The Maasai have lived in harmony with nature for generations, and now the job of conservationists is to see that the land, the animals, and all the people can live together.

9

Maybe we don't realize how important plants and animals are to our lives, but the Maasai can't forget them. Their lives are interconnected.

I guess some people think that the Maasai should just live in cities or towns, but if they did, their language and traditions could disappear. I hear Kisululu talk and know that the people are worried.

This morning, I woke up to the sight of the sun rising, creeping over the grass like a ball of fire. The higher it rose, the bluer the sky became.

Lions sat by the waterhole, and elephants were there too. It's odd to see predator and prey side by side. When the lions are full, they don't hunt. Soon it will be too hot for the lions, so they will find shade under the trees and sleep until it's a bit cooler.

This morning, the breeze carried Kisululu's voice into our house, which is shaped like a loaf of bread and made from bentwood. It is part of a whole circle of houses here in the village.

"Old and young must live together," Kisululu says. "As with plant and animal, each gives the other a place and a reason to be. To know how to protect the Earth, you have to know how to protect your family. It is good what you're doing."

My parents went off to talk, and I heard their voices rise and fall like the song of the grasshoppers as I drifted back to sleep.

When I woke up, my parents were gone. I walked outside, being careful to avoid the thorny branches that had been placed around the house. These branches keep wild animals out, and they do a good job, except for the snakes—like cobras, black mambas, and adders that can slither their way around them.

Kisululu handed me a gourd full of milk. I drank from it as I drank in the view. Only a few kinds of trees live here, like the acacia and the baobob. I've also seen wonderful animals in their natural habitats, like the tall giraffe and the secretary bird. Fruit bats fly from a nearby baobob tree at night, their flapping wings making an eerie sound. I watch ostriches run through the grass.

I have seen many peculiar sights here, including leopards and cheetahs and the gazelles they hunt. I have seen lions hunt zebra and wildebeest, and have felt the Earth tremble as herds of impala run from hunting dogs.

When I first saw this place, I said to my mother, "It is a sea of grass. When the wind blows through it, I feel as if I'm riding the waves."

There has been so much to get used to here—the sights, the sounds, the smells, and the tastes, but the hardest thing has been my not knowing anyone, and having no one know me.

So when I saw the bus rolling through a cloud of dust, I ran toward it. I ran because it carried my parents to me, and as I got closer, I saw a hand rubbing caked dust off the window. I couldn't see a face, just the hand, and still my stomach dropped to my toes. Then my heart began to dance.

The bus stopped and the doors opened. Out climbed my mother and my father, each carrying suitcases. Then at the top of the steps I saw my grandfather whose face was lit up with a smile. I felt mine do the same.

"Surprise!" everyone shouted.

"So this is why you've been gone all day!" I shouted as I danced with joy.

"We know you've been feeling sad lately and missing home. We thought it might help if we brought a piece of home here to you," my mom said.

"It was actually Kisululu's idea," my dad added. "We can learn from the people who have lived on this land for many years. They made room for us and for your grandfather too."

As I hugged my grandfather, I knew I would have new stories to tell and retell about my new home—my own sea of grass.